I0521249

Storylandia

The Wapshott Journal of Fiction

Issue 23

The Wapshott Press

Storylandia, Issue 23, The Wapshott Journal of Fiction, ISSN 1947-5349, ISBN 978-1-942007-15-9 is published at intervals by the Wapshott Press, now a 501(c)(3) nonprofit, PO Box 31513, Los Angeles, California, 90031-0513, telephone 323-201-7147. All correspondence can be sent to The Wapshott Press, PO Box 31513, LA CA 90031-0513. Visit our website at www.WapshottPress.org to learn more. This work is copyright © 2017 by Storylandia. The Wapshott Journal of Fiction, Los Angeles, California. Copyright © 2017 Fred Skolnik and is reprinted here with the copyright owner's permission.

Storylandia is always seeking quality original short stories, novelettes, and novellas. Please have a look at our submission guidelines at www.Storylandia.WapshottPress. org or email the editor at editor@wapshottpress.org

The Wapshott Press wishes to express our deepest gratitude to John Griogair Bell for the proofread and editorial support. John is a libraian at the Hermetic Library (https://hermetic.com/)

Cover: "Hubble's Bright Shining Lizard Star." by NASA.gov

ACKNOWLEDGMENTS

Daily Life in Ancient America – Children, Churches & Daddies, vol, 224, Jan. 2011

From the Minutes of the 458,734th Meeting of the Intergalactic Exploration Society – Commonline, Aug. 2015

Another Kind of Harmony – Sonar4, Fall 2009 (writing as Fred Skolnik)

Storylandia

The Wapshott Journal of Fiction

Founded in 2009

Issue 23, Autumn 2017

Edited by Ginger Mayerson

Aerial Views
Three Sci-Fi Satires
By Fred Russell

Table of Contents

In memory of Ada Steinberg
scholar, teacher, friend

Aerial Views

Three Sci-Fi Satires

By Fred Russell

DAILY LIFE IN ANCIENT AMERICA

(From a Report to the Intergalactic Exploration Society)

The planet Earth, as we all know, is the third body in the so-called solar system of the galaxy referred to by its former inhabitants as the Milky Way. That there are similar systems throughout this galaxy is common knowledge. The current report sums up the fifth season of excavations on this dead planet, confining itself to the region known in local parlance as "America," or, in other sources, "the United States of America." And while the primitive beings who populated this region are no different in essential features from those who inhabited other regions of the planet, our finds have made it possible to speculate more boldly about a number of questions that have occupied researchers for eons. These concern, first and foremost: 1) the age-old question of a possible evolutionary link between these beings and ourselves, as farfetched as such a link has always seemed, given the enormous distance and span of time that separate us; 2) the relationship between the two species of intelligent life uncovered on the planet; 3) the relationship between these species and the drones who served them in the peculiar society that prevailed there.

The chief inhabitants, and certainly the rulers, of the planet Earth can best be described, in physical terms, as rather squat in appearance and possessing a single large eye which was apparently the seat of their intelligence. It was through this all-seeing eye that the activities of the servile drones were monitored and controlled, the latter being instructed minutely and continuously in everything that pertained to their lives. Fortunately we are in possession of both written and recorded materials relating to both masters and slaves and can now decipher their primitive language, or at least the language by which masters and slaves communicated with one another if not among themselves. This is largely a result of the work done on the thousands of so-called Coca-Cola cans now housed in the Museum of Galactic History and displaying a variety of scripts that have been definitively collated and furnished our first insight into the structure of the American language. Having ascertained that the cans contained an acidic liquid that the drones were instructed to imbibe, conceivably as a means of pacifying them, researchers were able to decipher two words—"drink" and "refreshes"—that in effect made it possible to arrive at a full understanding of the system of meanings attached to the various combinations of symbols in this language.

Another question pertains to the dating of the various strata unearthed on American soil. We know that the American civilization flourished around 500,000 years ago. The Americans themselves, in the documents we have discovered, refer to what they call the 21st century as a pivotal time in their unfortunate history. However, there was apparently a zero year at which the count was reversed for an unknown reason, so it is unclear whether this refers to the 21st century before or after the zero year. In the former case the Americans would have antedated the people known as the Romans as a planetary power; in the latter case they would have followed them, and we shall allow ourselves to speculate about what contact, if any, these two civilizations had.

As for the relationship between the two species of intelligent life uncovered on the planet, though both flourished in America at around the same time it remains unclear whether one evolved from the other or simply destroyed the other. One school of thought maintains that the two species coupled and thus gave rise to yet a third species, to which we owe our own ultimate design. We shall discuss this question in greater detail later on in the Report.

For the present let it be said that the first

of these two species, known as Console I, strikes researchers as the more primitive of the two. The fortuitous discovery of the so-called Console Memory Disks allows us to view its thought processes as well as to observe the drones in various activities and to study the system of instructions by which they were controlled. On these disks, the drones themselves may be viewed performing the actions and speaking the words dictated to them by their masters as mirrored in the latter's all-seeing eye. Thus in one of these disks drones are seen drinking the aforesaid Coca-Cola beverage while feigning enjoyment in order to encourage others to do so. Females of the species with long, bare legs are gathered around the drinkers to create the illusion that drinking Coca-Cola leads to successful interfacing. Many of these tranquilizing drugs are administered to the drones as they perform their tasks. Occasionally they are seen gathered around the console to receive further instructions.

As for the second of these two species, Console II, this was no doubt an advanced type vis-à-vis Console I, though as mentioned before their precise relationship is difficult to define. Certainly they coexisted for a brief period, whether in harmony or strife it is also difficult to ascertain. That both were continually engaged in war can be seen by even the most cursory review of the disks. Console I in particular reveals images of the most violent nature, apparently sending armies of drones around the planet to do his bidding. Occasionally some of these drones achieved a measure of prominence among their own kind and are displayed being put through their paces, sometimes hitting a ball with a stick, sometimes jumping up and down in an enthusiastic manner.

Console II seems to have been a more subtle creature, performing what must have been regarded at the time as complex mental tasks which were displayed in its eye. The transparency of these mental processes, or at least the immediate results, is one of the features that distinguishes this early form of life. Console II was always thinking, but also always observing, its eye jumping from place to place in search of information and often engaged in "creative" activities.

As for the drones, they were less compactly made and put together out of inferior materials that could not be recycled. They possessed the aforementioned "legs" to transport them from place to place and "arms" for snatching things out of the air which they then guarded jealously. Planted atop this nexus of appendages was a globular mass that contained two small eyes with which they surveyed their surroundings and an active mouth generally engaged in the acts of eating or talking. They were by and large incapable of thinking for themselves and hence, as mentioned, had to be instructed continuously.

So much for the broad features of the creatures who inhabited the planet Earth in that distant time when intelligent life was not yet self-sustaining. Of the beginnings of the consoles little is known, though a still more primitive creature has been identified from a somewhat earlier time which by no stretch of the imagination can be called intelligent. It too was squat and boxlike but unlike Console I and Console II could project no images, making instead sounds that mimicked speech but cannot be said to reflect any processes of thought, though some have argued, quite controversially, it may be added, that Console I evolved from it, just as it is said that Console II evolved from Console I.

Be that as it may, and irregardless of where we place Console I and Console II in our time frame or how we perceive their evolution, we find the consoles always engaged in three principal activities: the making of war, the accumulation of wealth and the control and manipulation of the drones. In America these activities reached a pinnacle of sorts in the aforementioned 21st century, not long before the series of catastrophes that put an end to this ill-fated civilization. At the time of which we are speaking America was ruled by a group of individuals known as "producers." These determined the content of the messages transmitted to the drones. It should be pointed out that though the drones cannot be characterized as intelligent beings, their role in this civilization was paramount, for it was they who performed the tasks on which it was founded, including the making of war, while themselves being dependent on the instructions they received from their masters, being incapable of acting without such instructions and having to be frequently reminded of them, such as in the case of the need to drink Coca-Cola in order to maintain their mental equilibrium.

These producers, while thought of collectively as a group, were often at odds among themselves and apparently competed fiercely to achieve positions of power, even to the extent of sending out contradictory messages to the drones. For example, each of the producers instructed the drones to imbibe different kinds of acidic beverages or to think different kinds of thoughts, employing prominent drones to endorse these messages and thus deceive the general drone population into believing that it was admirable to obey them and that they would furthermore be rewarded in some indeterminate way, perhaps by becoming prominent themselves.

Our good fortune in obtaining fairly complete individuals of both the Console I and Console II types as well as a large number of memory disks, all on view at the Galactic Museum of Natural History, has given us, as mentioned, a rare opportunity to study their thought processes as well as the behavior of the drones. When the drones were left to their own devices, that is, not receiving messages or doing their masters' bidding, they were generally engaged in conflicts among themselves, many of which were resolved violently. It can only be surmised that their masters viewed these proceedings with a certain measure of amusement and conceivably were in the habit of observing them as a form of entertainment. In a typical spectacle of this sort one of the male drones would be seen pursuing a female drone with long, bare legs and occasionally interfacing with her. When another male drone appeared on the scene one would inevitably destroy the other. All this heated activity was regulated by instructing the drones to imbibe pacifying beverages at certain intervals.

The consoles we have investigated are of a more or less uniform design and nature. All have mysterious cords or cables hanging from their bodies which are conceivably sex organs used in interfacing, though this conclusion has been challenged by a number of researchers who believe they are feeding appendages. In truth it is not precisely known how the consoles interfaced or nurtured themselves. More advanced beings have no need for appendages to interface or feed but like us are part of a central processing unit in which interfacing and feeding are automatically achieved. Among the drones, of course, the system was even more primitive, with interfacing performed by pinning females on the ground.

When the consoles were first interfaced with our own system in a bold experiment carried out here at the Society, a measure of mental activity was detected but none that could be defined. In the case of Console I a turbulent field of some kind was produced in its eye. In the case of Console II a series of colorful boxes or logos was produced against varying backgrounds. Our preliminary conclusion was that this activity represented a state of somnolence. It was only when we inserted the recently discovered memory disks that both came to life and began to yield their fascinating secrets. These will be discussed at length later on. For the moment I will describe just three of them:

Disk 12, Console I Series, shows a drone reading messages which are interspersed with views of other drones in varying states of excitement and by instructions urging the drones to dye their hair. Towards the end of this presentation the reader drone is replaced by a female drone with long, bare legs reciting mysterious numbers.

Disk 84, Console I Series, shows a number of drones sitting around a table telling the general drone population what to think and describing future events. For example, at the beginning of the disk, the first drone describes what a producer in America will say to a producer in "Europe" when the two meet at a later date to discuss the future of the planet and the second drone describes what the European producer will reply. A third drone discusses the significance of this imaginary conversation. On many points the drones are in disagreement and therefore raise their voices to make a stronger impression on the ordinary drones waiting to be instructed.

Disk 243, Console I Series, shows a drone sitting at a desk and various prominent drones reporting to him and replying to questions. After each reply the drone at the desk laughs heartily pretending it was the wittiest reply he had ever heard and thus encouraging large numbers of unseen drones to join in the laughter. Between these exchanges messages are transmitted instructing the general drone population to eat fried chicken.

It can be surmised that the engagement of the drones in the manner depicted in these disks was intended to keep them occupied lest they engage in violent activities, such as destroying one another or pinning females on the ground. As previously mentioned, the general drone population was controlled by the consoles designated "producers." In the time of which we are speaking, the leader of the American producer consoles was generally referred to as George Bush though occasionally—and significantly—as George W. Bush as well. We find the former name in records of the Earth years 1992 and 2000 and this accords with the generally accepted notion that the lifespan of Console I was just eight years before recycling or upgrading. This is indirectly supported by the colloquial American expression "the mind of an eight-year-old" occasionally encountered in the texts, especially with reference to the said George Bush. A particularly intriguing thesis has recently been advanced arguing that the console known as George Bush and the console known as George Washington were identical, the proper designation of the former thus being George Washington Bush. This would explain the mystery of the letter W occasionally encountered in the George Bush designation. The fact that the only Earth year associated in the records with this George Washington is 1792 would seem to bear out this argument, as clearly a scribal error would have occurred, substituting the number 7 for the number 9. If then this George Washington Bush flourished toward the end of the 20th century it may be suggested that the Roman and American civilizations were contemporaneous and the wars previously believed to have been fought between the Romans and the "Persians" or "Parthians" were in fact fought against the Americans, who "crossed the Delaware" (that is, the Tigris) and toppled the statue of the Roman leader in his capital city after dropping heavy objects on the heads of its inhabitants. It is through such ingenious syntheses that our understanding of ancient history is largely derived.

As stated, the American wars were fought by its drone population. However, in addition to destroying one another and pinning females on the ground the drones also engaged in a peculiar activity best described as the acquisition of commodities. In such transactions these commodities were distributed to the drones in exchange for quantities of paper known as "money." The circulation of this money, like everything else in this society, was controlled by the producers, who apparently made a limited amount available to the general drone population while keeping the bulk of it for themselves. Among the drones too there were considerable disparities in the amounts of money thus received. Those who were adept at hitting a ball with a stick or jumping up and down, for example, received much more of this money than those whom the producers enlisted to fight their wars. Many theories have been advanced to explain the principles that governed the distribution of commodities in America, as there is no apparent logic in the disparities characterizing this distribution and it cannot be explained rationally why hitting a ball with a stick or jumping up and down was considered more admirable, for example, than cleaning toilets or collecting garbage, not to mention fighting wars. Among other things, it has been argued that the distribution of commodities among various classes of drones was made on a random basis, one group or another being given preference in a given time. Thus it is said that while hitting a ball with a stick was greatly admired in the 20th century it was considered a somewhat puerile occupation in previous centuries, engaged in only by children or the mentally defective. This has not been proven conclusively but as a theory it has much to commend it.

Still another theory maintains that commodities were distributed according to a color code, with drones colored white receiving a greater proportion of commodities than drones colored black, for example, unless the latter were adept at hitting a ball with a stick or jumping up and down. It is not known how the allotment of these colors was determined or why they might have been chosen as a criterion for distributing commodities. The Console I disks display many of these black-colored drones being apprehended by white-colored drones wearing odd hats and sometimes also hitting them with a stick. It is conceivable that these are the same sticks used for hitting balls but there is no evidence to indicate that the white-colored drones were rewarded for hitting black-colored drones to the same extent as for hitting balls and it must therefore be concluded that the white-colored drones engaged in this activity for simple pleasure.

As mentioned, the drones were encouraged to acquire commodities through messages mirrored in the all-seeing eye of Console I or Console II and clearly displayed in the memory disks we have obtained. The supply of these commodities seems to have been unlimited but, as we have pointed out, the amount of "money" available for the purpose of acquiring them was not. It can only be concluded that the tactic of "teasing" the drones by offering them what they could not obtain must have had a deleterious effect on their mental state. Why this was done is not altogether clear. Inevitably it would have produced unrest among the drone population and even attempts to obtain these commodities without the said money, that is by seizing them, just as many were in the habit of seizing females with long, bare legs and pinning them on the ground for the purpose of interfacing. Many researchers have attempted to tie together these many and diverse peculiarities to present a coherent picture of how this society functioned, but with little success. The central motifs of this society—endless wars, unobtainable commodities, females with long, bare legs, hitting balls with sticks and drinking Coca-Cola—do not add up to anything that resembles a rational social order.

The consoles were housed in lodgings of various kinds together with the drones who served them, generally four or five in number, though producer consoles were understandably served by a great many more and were therefore lodged in much larger abodes. The consoles began issuing their instructions and monitoring the drones early in the morning. A female drone was generally instructed to prepare a beverage called "coffee." To encourage her to do so the consoles displayed prominent drones imbibing the said beverage as they sat around a table chatting amiably and frequently laughing. A full-grown male drone, sometimes barely dressed and often scratching himself, then appeared and was served the coffee. In some cases the male and female interfaced, but generally on these occasions the female was not pinned on the ground. It may be that this "coffee" prevented the drones from interfacing too violently at unpropitious times. Smaller drones often joined the full-grown ones and imbibed various nutrients while images projected in the all-seeing eye of the console, most often in the form of "morality tales," also reminded them to uphold the values deemed by the consoles to be the most beneficial to themselves. The drones were furthermore instructed to engage in gainful employment in the service of the consoles, for which, as we have suggested, they were paradoxically "rewarded" by being allotted small amounts of "money" with which to obtain the less valuable of the commodities which they themselves produced while the consoles used the bulk of the money to augment their material wealth and conduct their wars. The consoles observed the drones very closely during these morning preparations and made certain that they got out of the house on time to perform their allotted tasks. Though Console I was a primitive being possessing limited intelligence, one cannot but admire the ingenious manner in which he was able to manipulate the hapless drones.

It is not always clear how the gainful employment in which the drones were engaged served the interests of the consoles. While it is clear that drones were needed to fight the wars of the consoles, it is less clear why they were required to produce such a bewildering variety of acidic beverages. We have no reason to believe that these beverages differed from one another in any essential way or served any essential purpose other than pacifying the drones, in which case one such beverage would have sufficed. One theory maintains that it was not the production of commodities per se but the generation of economic "activity" as such that was the primary objective, and in fact "interests" in often imaginary commodities were traded back and forth with the sole purpose of accruing "money." Those among the drones who accrued money in this manner were often more prominent than drones who excelled at hitting a ball with a stick or jumping up and down and were held up to ordinary drones as positive examples by the producers, who encouraged them to believe that any drone could become prominent and that it was therefore in their own best interests to be gainfully employed and continue to manufacture and consume acidic beverages. In this way a measure of harmony was apparently achieved which allowed the consoles to rule their domains and pursue their interests in relative peace and security.

The consoles occupied a central space in their abodes while the drones were sent hither and yon to perform their tasks. Frequently the drones were called together and clustered around the consoles to receive messages or instructions, entering what appears to be a hypnotic state, perhaps induced by the tranquilizing beverages they were encouraged to imbibe. These were generally protracted sessions, lasting hours in

Earth time, as the drones were apparently slow to comprehend what was required of them and therefore each message had to be repeated many times.

The eyes of the consoles were everywhere. Mirrored there were shifting scenes as the drones were monitored from one end of the Earth to the other. As stated before, in addition to allowing the consoles to "keep an eye" on things, these scenes no doubt served to entertain the consoles as well. Apparently nothing amused them more than watching the drones destroy one another and pin females with long, bare legs on the ground. It is also conceivable that the drones summoned to receive instructions were meant to be mesmerized by these scenes as much as by drinking their tranquilizing beverages and therefore made more receptive to the messages being transmitted to them. Sometimes, after observing such scenes, the assembled drones also pinned females on the ground or attempted to destroy one another, though this could not have been the intention of the consoles, whose purpose was to instruct the drones in their ordinary tasks and encourage them to acquire commodities. Conceivably these violent scenes were the "price" the consoles had to pay to maintain the drones in a hypnotic state and thereby hold their attention, though as mentioned before the end result of this policy was to frustrate the drones since the most desirable of the commodities they were encouraged to acquire were unobtainable as were the most desirable of the females with long, bare legs displayed in the all-seeing eye of the consoles so that many of the drones were brought to a state of frenzied excitation and pinned on the ground any female that came along.

It is not clear whether or to what extent the producer consoles also controlled the ordinary consoles, who were apparently delegated to monitor and instruct the drones at what might be called the local level. The truth is, we have no way of distinguishing among consoles of either the Console I or Console II type, just as we have no way of distinguishing among drones, other than recognizing that some were ordinary and some prominent. All we can say for certain, aside from noting the activities that characterized each species, is that commodities were divided among them in a particular way, favoring the prominent. Thus, if we take the ratio that obtained between the drone and console populations as four to one on the basis of archeological evidence, and the division of wealth in the reverse proportion in accordance with the General Theory of Economic Inequality that prevailed in America at the time, we may conclude that twenty percent of the American population controlled eighty percent of its wealth and that the latter was divided among the consoles in accordance with their status, the producers naturally receiving a larger share, though, in the well-known American phrase, "there was more than enough to go around."

The manner in which certain consoles became producers and exercised control over money, commodities and the minds of the drones is also not altogether clear. Some researchers argue that, in the main, such producers "seized" power in much the same way as the drones themselves sometimes seized females and pinned them on the ground. This manner of seizing power was the subject of many of the "morality tales" devised by the consoles to pacify the drones. In these tales the seizure of power and the possession of wealth are most often represented as villainous while paradoxically the acquisition of commodities is promoted as the highest good. It is clear that the intention is to discourage the drones from seizing power and accumulating wealth in the manner of the consoles while at the same time "compensating" the drones by allowing them to experience a sense of moral satisfaction. Maintenance of the famous four-to-one ratio laid down in the General Theory of Economic Inequality, which seems to have been elevated to the status of a universal principle, was apparently paramount in preserving the social order prevalent in America at the time we are discussing.

The manner of seizing and maintaining power, however, is not always represented as forcible. Often subtle means were employed to cause the drones to bend to the will of the producers. We have mentioned mesmerization through the repeated transmission of messages endorsed by prominent drones in the company of females with long, bare legs. Often, too, the drones were promised a greater share of commodities or that fewer of them would be slaughtered in the wars periodically conducted by the consoles. Drones were occasionally urged to "vote" for consoles who made such promises, and this perhaps was the manner in which some of them became producers, though most of them clearly relied on their own devices. Those "elected" occupied "seats of government" but clearly acted in collusion with other producer consoles, devising various schemes to manipulate or pacify the drones and enhance their own power and wealth.

It has been asked how basically immobile creatures such as the consoles could have exercised such a hold on the relatively mobile drones who in effect had it in their power to smash them to smithereens and seize power for themselves as had occasionally occurred in other localities on the face of the Earth. The most obvious answer is that they were too stupid to do so and that is why they remained drones while their masters evolved into consoles with remarkable manipulative skills, even enlisting the drones to police themselves as well as to fight their wars while dangling before them visions of wealth and prominence that were in effect attainable by only a chosen few. Those picked out of the great mass of drones that gathered around the consoles hoping to be chosen were immediately separated from the others and elevated to podiums and stages from which they could look out on ordinary drones with a clear sense of superiority and were even applauded if not idolized by the drones left behind.

As mentioned, the duplication of commodities with minute variations to make them seem "different" was intended to stimulate economic activity and enable the producers to augment their wealth. In the peculiar economic system that prevailed in America and in other parts of the planet, such wealth was most often intangible, consisting of "interests" or "shares" in facilities whose value was calculated in accordance with the presumed ability of their owners to persuade the drones to acquire the commodities or services they produced, irrespective of whether such commodities or services had any useful or essential purpose. When such facilities failed to live up to expectations, this wealth often dissolved, but those who controlled them were generally wily enough to "squeeze them dry" and leave others "holding the bag." The existence of such an abundance of colorful phrases in the American language to describe the manner in which these creatures habitually "screwed" one another in economic transactions is a clear indication of the moral climate of this society.

As mentioned, the criminal activities of the consoles were often the subject of the morality tales shown to the drones to keep them in line. In these morality tales the consoles were portrayed by drones serving as "actors." The actor drones pretended to be consoles, aping their speech and mannerisms though obvious physical limitations prevented them from assuming the actual appearance of the consoles despite the ingenious attempts sometimes made to "dress up" the drones to look like otherworldly creatures. The actor drones also portrayed ordinary and prominent drones and these were often pitted against the consoles to highlight the moral point of the tale. Thus an actor drone might portray a "banker" console "evicting" downtrodden drones from their homes or employing a "lawyer" to steal what little money they had. The console might also be portrayed pinning a female with long, bare legs on the ground, all the while flashing menacing or triumphant looks and clearly being cast as the villain of the piece. These villains were inevitably overcome by a drone "hero" who was rewarded by himself being allowed to pin a desirable female on the ground, though often they were only seen interfacing in a standing position, the rest being left to the imagination of the drones gathered around the consoles during the evening hours to receive their messages and instructions. That these were only "tales" meant to instruct the drones is evident from the fact that these same bankers were honored figures in console society and, like the prominent drones, held up as examples of "success" to the drones, who were urged to emulate them within the bounds of the laws enacted by the consoles and aspire to the acquisition of the commodities produced by them.

Though the actor drones who portrayed the heroes in these tales lacked the skills of even the most ordinary drones and were only adept at pretending to be heroes, they became prominent themselves and were rewarded with an abundance of commodities, some of which they endorsed to encourage ordinary drones to acquire them. In our disks, as mentioned before, they are often seen reporting to drones sitting behind desks and making witty replies to the questions they are asked, causing the drone behind the desk to laugh heartily. Sometimes they even sing songs. All are apparently endowed with a quality referred to as "personality" which sets them apart from such ordinary drones as teachers and farmers and nurses, for example, and elevates them to the heights occupied by those who excel at hitting a ball with a stick or jumping up and down.

The drones sitting behind the desks are meant to be perceived as witty fellows themselves and also endowed with "personality" and often come out from behind their desks and tell amusing stories to the unseen drones who comprise what is called the "studio audience." Members of this studio audience also laugh heartily when instructed to, as do the unseen drones gathered around the consoles in their homes. On the other hand, there is little laughter in those presentations where a drone reads messages interspersed with views of drones in varying states of excitement. These are solemn occasions, often depicting drones who have destroyed other drones and sometimes depicting the destroyed drones themselves lying on the pavement with a bullet in their heads. A female with long, bare legs generally describes the scene and reappears in the all-seeing eye of the console each time a significant detail can be added to the saga, such as what the victim ate for breakfast that day or where he had planned to go on vacation. This is known as "live" coverage though as often as not it deals with the dead.

As also mentioned, prominent drones are often shown sitting around a table discoursing at length about various subjects, the object being, as we have said, to instruct ordinary drones in what they should think and to create a suitable framework in which acidic beverages and other commodities can be sold. Some of these prominent drones are called "journalists" and some are called "professors." Some are called "analysts" and some are called "experts." How the drones earn these designations and the fine distinctions among them is something of a mystery. It has been suggested that all these "talkers" are distinguished by degree of learning, the analysts and journalists being somewhat more ignorant than the experts and professors. This is borne out by the fact that while the analysts and journalists are forever predicting future events they seldom predict them correctly and are no more capable of knowing what will occur in a week or a month than they are capable of knowing what will occur in the next five minutes, though the same may be said of the experts and professors. The question has been asked how these creatures exercise such mesmerizing powers and are able to keep hordes of drones "glued" to the consoles and hanging on every word when even ordinary drones know that such talk is without meaning or value. The stupidity of the drone has already been noted. It has also been suggested that these "talk shows" are forms of entertainment rather than forums for instruction, the clash of views creating "dramas" on the model of the more violent clashes the drones enjoy watching. It may even be said that these "shows" achieve a kind of esthetic effect, "putting into words" what the ignorant drones "feel" but cannot express in the polished language of the experts and analysts. Each drone thus identifies with a given expert or analyst who reflects his own prejudices, mindlessly repeating his half-truths and constructing out of them a "credo" of dogmatic views that remain embedded in his mind for an entire lifetime like bricks in a brick wall. As a theory, this perhaps goes too far. It is more likely that the drones are simply habituated into craving instant "news" and "analysis" just as they are habituated into craving Coca-Cola. Thus, in this spirit, if the secrets of the universe were about to be revealed by God Himself, the broadcast might be interrupted to bring the drones "live coverage" of a ten-car pileup on the Los Angeles Freeway.

The prominent drones who consent to appear in such productions and "air" their views, migrating from talk show to talk show like "medieval" jesters, are rewarded by being "seen" and this no doubt serves as a form of self-gratification comparable to what is referred to in our society as auto-degradation, that is, interfacing with oneself. The urge to talk publicly and express views on every subject under the sun was a particular disease of this society, known as "running off at the mouth." There was no known cure. Wherever the drones turned someone was always talking at them, sometimes to manipulate them, sometimes to pacify them, sometimes to instruct them, sometimes to entertain them.

The drones, for their part, sat quietly around the consoles drinking Coca-Cola and stuffing themselves with salted peanuts and potato chips. Many were perverse and did not follow their instructions immediately, sinking into a state of somnolence while the prominent drones in the all-seeing eye of the consoles harangued them to go out and buy breakfast cereals and "lite" beer, only doing so the following day when they went "shopping." The shopping centers designed by the consoles for this purpose were staffed by drones like themselves who were paid what was called "the minimum wage" and therefore did their own "shopping" in degraded establishments located especially for them among empty warehouses and burned-out buildings. Some drones of course received no wages at all and were reduced to stealing, though in a considerably less sophisticated manner than the consoles who ruled them. Among thieves of the console variety there was apparently little honor, for rather than sharing their spoils with their partners in crime, they kept the bulk of these spoils for themselves, depleting the general wealth of the race through a variety of criminal devices subsumed under the all-encompassing heading of "making a killing." These included, among other things, such expedients as "grabbing land," "cornering markets," "fixing prices," "eliminating competitors," "laundering money," "greasing palms," "finding loopholes," and causing "shares" representing imaginary wealth to fluctuate wildly by buying and selling at opportune moments and in this way "cashing in." Drones without wages, generally color-coded black and lacking the higher education required to engage in fraud, embezzlement, tax evasion and insider trading, were forced to resort to such crude devices as snatching money out of cash registers.

As mentioned, Console II was an advanced version of Console I, employing different and no doubt more ingenious methods to monitor and instruct the drones. Whereas Console I required that the drones merely "sit still" during the process of instruction, Console II actively engaged the drones in a kind of dialogue to discover their thoughts, allowing them to "air" their opinions and resentments in much the same manner that prominent drones were allowed to hold forth on the talk shows and thereby deceiving them into believing that their words had weight. The opinions expressed by the drones were even less literate than those expressed by the journalists and riddled with the same inaccuracies, thereby lowering the level of public discourse even further. Ordinary drones searched the great memory banks of Console II and repeated the errors implanted there by the journalists while the journalists searched these same memory banks and repeated the errors implanted there by the ordinary drones. Console II also allowed the drones to indulge their various perversions, practice destroying one another in lively "games" and "shop" promiscuously with a simple click of a "mouse" while himself engaging in the elaboration of ever more sophisticated methods by which to mesmerize, monitor and regulate the drones.

As we have said, Console I and Console II coexisted for a time, presumably competing for the attention of the drones, with each controlling them after his own fashion. By the 22nd century Console I had all but disappeared from the historical record. The memory disks we have come to possess from that time all belong to Console II. We cannot confirm that they cohabited and that one species was absorbed by the other, as some have suggested. The females of the Console II variety had rather large ports especially engineered to receive the plugs sported by Console II males, making them perfect mates, if that was the intention, while Console I was a poorer "fit" despite the sometimes extraordinary length of the male cable. It is more likely that Console I males interfaced with Console I females and that Console II males interfaced with Console II females. Nor can we say that one destroyed the other. It is conceivable that Console I "died off" after a natural disaster created environmental conditions unfavorable to his survival while Console II was able to adapt and therefore flourished. In the burial sites where remains of Console I were found, known in local parlance as "garbage dumps," there are also remains of "household items" buried beside the consoles, making it clear that Console I believed in an afterlife, thinking to take these effects with him on the long journey to that other world. Traces of organic matter have also been found in these "garbage dumps," conceivably intended as sustenance for the journey. From the evidence of the Console I disks we may conclude that theirs was a primitive religion whose adherents were ministered to by ignorant preachers "interpreting" holy books whose original language they did not understand. The relationship between these preachers and their "flocks" was very much like the relationship between journalists and ordinary drones.

Drones were conditioned into the habit of obedience from an early age, being left in front of the consoles to receive instructions for hours at a time and soon being able to repeat their messages word for word much to the delight of the full-grown drones who cared for them and in this way were assured that the little ones were growing up to be useful members of society who would "fit in" and not "make waves." At a certain age the young drones began hitting a ball with a stick and jumping up and down and were encouraged to dream of becoming prominent. At a later age they began pinning females on the ground and practicing the art of destroying one another in the lively games made available to them by Console II. Some of them were thus eager to participate in the wars organized by the producer consoles, though others preferred to act alone and destroy rival drones on an individual or "pay-as-you-play" basis. In either case the producer consoles furnished them with high-power weapons, in this manner practicing an ingenious form of population control and not allowing the growth rate of the drones to get out of hand. This was known in democratic parlance as the system of checks and balances.

"Democracy" was the generic term for the political system by which the consoles controlled the drones and was hailed as superior to the systems by which other civilizations controlled their drones, most notably "dictatorship," where a single console determined everything in contrast to the more "enlightened" system of democracy where a few dozen or a few hundred consoles determined everything and the general drone population was given the illusion of ruling itself by being allowed to choose which of these consoles would control it directly. The consoles chosen in this way were generally those who spoke to the drones in the most polished language, had access to the most wealth, and had interfaced with the fewest females. If it was subsequently discovered that one of these "elected officials" had interfaced with a larger number of females than was considered seemly, or had even interfaced with other males, he was often made to retire in disgrace and give up his place to a more "moral" console. Journalists labeled "watchdogs of democracy" reported these transgressions diligently, if not avidly, under headlines big enough to announce a world war, thus protecting the public from "breaches of trust."

The title "watchdog of democracy" does not seem to have been earned through any particular course of studies or official certification but rather expropriated by the journalistic profession as a license to invade the privacy of anyone whose prominence might attract a large audience for the gossip, innuendo and calumny spread by the said journalists after consulting with batteries of lawyers to see what they could get away with. These journalists were for the most part solemn, if not smug, fellows, aiming to create the impression that as self-appointed watchdogs they were models of integrity and putting on a stern and disapproving look when they stood in front of a camera describing the transgressions of others. However, when real crimes were committed these journalists seldom reported them to the police but jealously guarded the information in order to produce a "scoop" and win the envy and admiration of their colleagues, if not of the entire drone population, and in this way further their careers.

Occasionally, it would seem, instead of being directly "elected," the "candidates" were required to run a "race," the winner automatically receiving the aforementioned "votes." It is not clear why prowess at running was thought to represent fitness for governing, as "running a race" would only determine who was the fastest. These races were apparently held in various localities and the candidate traditionally "spoke" while running, perhaps to demonstrate his versatility, or simply to entertain the "voters." From what we can make out from the memory disks nothing "spoken" by the candidates during these races had the slightest bearing on the way the country was governed. But as we have noted, the drones had been habituated into receiving instructions and messages and expected the consoles to talk to them even if it was gibberish. After these "races" the candidates were generally exhausted, like the drones after interfacing, and took vacations to recuperate.

Among other things, Americans were

instructed to believe that the American system of government was the best on Earth and were therefore determined to export it to other nations, even if they didn't want it. Thus, after "crossing the Tigris" in their war with the Romans and dropping heavy objects on the heads of anyone who happened to be in the vicinity "to soften them up," the Americans instituted "free elections." However, in the midst of this noble endeavor, they were surprised to discover that the various "camps" in the society they wished to transform were more intent on destroying one another, and the Americans as well, than on choosing consoles to manipulate and control them in the American tradition. The Americans countered this resistance by seizing "insurgents" and having them interrogated energetically through "interpreters." If "interpreters" were not available they found someone who spoke pidgin English to serve in their stead. The information thus gathered was evaluated by officials who understood neither the language nor the culture of the land they had "liberated." These officials sent "intelligence reports" to George Washington Bush and the officials who surrounded him, who also did not understand the language and the culture of the land they had liberated. On the basis of these reports Mr. Bush assessed the "mood" of the liberated country and calculated the probable course of future events, somewhat perplexed when it turned out that these calculations had neglected to allow for the loss of thousands of American lives, hundreds of thousands of local lives, and hundreds of billions of dollars without achieving anything that came close to the desired results, which were of course unattainable. "I'm a war president," Mr. Bush said. "I make war. That's what I do."

As it was the drones who were being killed in this war and not George Washington Bush and his officials or their sons and daughters, Mr. Bush was able to arrange a "surge," whose "positive" results were dutifully reported by the journalists "embedded" in combat units and having the time of their lives. The insane language invented by the consoles to bamboozle the drones was picked up by the journalists as though they had been speaking it all their lives. They became "war correspondents" and appeared before cameras wearing flak jackets and expressing their admiration for the "courageous men and women" being slaughtered in the name of freedom and democracy. When they got back home they were heroes themselves and told "war stories" to admiring females over drinks and consequently found that they were able to pin more of them on the ground than when they were reporting graft at City Hall. It may be noted parenthetically that the failure of reporters to report accurately and meaningfully is not necessarily a result of bad intentions, though they are of course eager "to make a splash." Most often it is a result of lack of talent, for if they could see deeper or write better they would not be reporters, they would be historians and even novelists. Let us now ask ourselves how the consoles became consoles and the drones became drones.

If the origins of the consoles are shrouded in mystery, all the more so are the origins of the drones. The generally held theory is that they evolved from a race of monkeys. Given their general appearance, their lack of intelligence and their habit, as it is put in their own language, of "aping" the behavior taught to them by the consoles, there is much in this theory to commend it. However, glimpses of these monkeys, or their near kin, which we get from the memory disks at our disposal, prove conclusively that the monkeys were a relatively advanced form of life compared with the drones and certainly more intelligent. For one thing they did not allow their troops to be herded into platoons, companies and regiments by the consoles for the purpose of making war and being periodically slaughtered, nor did they consent to imbibe the Coca-Cola beverage employed by the consoles to pacify the drones and make them incapable of resistance to their messages and instructions. Conceivably the consoles punished the monkeys for their intransigence by putting them "behind bars" just as they punished the drones in a like manner for interfacing too violently or destroying one another without receiving instructions to do so from the consoles, not to mention grabbing money from cash registers. In any case, monkeys seldom destroyed one another, which in itself is a sure sign of superior intelligence vis-à-vis the drones, and for the most part led a peaceful existence munching fruit or berries with an occasional handful of nuts as a special treat.

The theory that the drones, a regressive species, evolved from the monkeys is therefore highly questionable. If anything, it might be said that the monkeys evolved from the drones, and from here, through a great leap of the imagination, one might even venture to suggest that the consoles evolved from the monkeys. I will remind you that we have in our possession a very ancient text that speaks of a so-called "proconsul" ancestor monkey, and the similarity of this nomenclature to that of the consoles hardly needs to be emphasized. Is this mere coincidence, or can it be argued that "proconsul" should be read "proconsole"? It may be pointed out at this juncture that the remains of primates even older than "proconsul" or "proconsole" have been discovered in Ancient America, some with 44 "teeth," some with 36. This measure of their "processing" capacity is highly reminiscent of the so-called "megabytes" used as a measure in Console II and strengthens the evolutionary argument even further. In this context the American expression "to make a monkey" out of someone, namely a drone, is highly significant, though we do not believe that drones were "made" into monkeys overnight, as it were, but evolved into monkeys over a considerable length of time, losing in the process many of their more primitive features. Thus, while monkeys often jumped up and down and ran around in circles, and even occasionally hit a ball with a stick, and it might have occurred to the consoles to toss them a few peanuts occasionally in the way of a reward, such monkeys never achieved a special status among their fellows like the drones who excelled at such displays, for clearly the general monkey population was too wise to be taken in by them, having better things to do with its time than standing around and watching a bunch of monkeys making fools out of themselves. In this context it is noteworthy that while a certain species of monkey, the "gorilla," often struck himself on the breast in a vestigial display of drone behavior he never went so far as to leap high in the air and bounce his body against the bodies of other gorillas.

We do not wish to overstate our case. The jury is still out, so to speak, on the question of whether the monkeys evolved from the drones or the drones from the monkeys. Clearly they coexisted, just as Console I and Console II coexisted, and clearly it was the drones whom the consoles chose to enslave as a kind of domestic animal, organizing this lowly class into a hierarchy of "orders," at the pinnacle of which stood the "talkers" and entertainers. Clearly these orders evolved over a long period of time though it is not known how and when the consoles gained control of them. The consoles themselves, whether they evolved from monkeys or the "talking" boxes that apparently antedated them, also have a long history. Indeed, when we use the term "history" we are in effect speaking only about the events associated with these rulers of the planet. Properly speaking, slaves do not have a history. They are only instruments of history, driven by their masters.

Though the consoles were divided into producer consoles and ordinary consoles it would be incorrect to speak of console orders in the same way that we speak of drone orders. The consoles in effect constituted a single order, that of rulers, with circumstance rather than ability determining which of them became producers. Nor did every console even wish to become a producer. Some apparently preferred to remain "behind the scenes." In any case, each had his own domain, and while competition was often fierce among them, the important task of controlling the drones was never neglected. No matter which console prevailed the messages and instructions never stopped coming, and since the end result was the same and one way or the other the drones did their shopping and showed up for the wars, it really didn't matter who was in charge.

It is conceivable that the drones did not fully understand that they had been enslaved by the consoles. In fact, more often than not, they insisted they were free, and this is again a tribute to the skill of the consoles in creating a potent arsenal of rhetorical and subliminal devices with which to confound and manipulate the drones. The consoles were not only "strongmen," they were also master psychologists. The drone therefore always believed that he wanted to do what he was instructed to do and the console could therefore always claim that he was giving the drone what the drone had asked for, such as Coca-Cola after addicting him to it with mountains of caffeine and sugar, or "breaking news" after addicting him to ultimate or apocalyptic spectacles. Giving the drone what he appeared to want was known as the "democratic argument," as opposed to the "elitism" of those who claimed the drone was being fed garbage. Sipping Coca-Cola and watching shootouts at the neighborhood high school, the drone believed he was living the good life.

This good life consisted of accumulating commodities and achieving a level of physical comfort comparable to that of the hippopotamus wallowing in mud at the local zoo. But while the mind of the hippopotamus was generally at ease, the mind of the drone was often agitated. The moment the console released him and he was "on his own" the drone was apt to dwell on his condition. This was known as "taking stock." Often he was forced to conclude that his inventories were not at the desired level and that there was little he could do about it. Often his basic level of physical comfort was in jeopardy. Always he looked out toward the horizon and saw other drones "getting ahead" and scaling the heights tantalizingly mirrored in the all-seeing eye of the consoles. This caused not a little distress, for which the remedies offered by the consoles—drugs, alcohol, cigarettes, soft drinks, fattening foods, therapy and nonstop entertainment—were not enough. The drone was often at least mildly depressed, his moods swung up and down, and occasionally he ran the risk of going through the ceiling or falling through the floor. Some became homeless, others went insane.

However, it cannot be denied that for a time a certain equilibrium was maintained in American society as a whole, though occasionally the consoles tested its resiliency by "diluting" the wealth at the lower end even further and allowing more and more drones to drop through the bottom. Though the result was a rise in violent crime, the consoles were able to contain it by creating vast inner city "reserves" for the violent or indigent while the more fortunate drones were able to ignore it by closing themselves off in "gated" communities. Among the consoles there was considerable debate about how far the existing model could be stretched, that is, how much crime and poverty could be tolerated without disturbing the sleep of the consoles. Some believed that it was possible to have as little as ten percent of the population controlling as much as ninety percent of the wealth and one percent controlling fifty percent, as long as the instructions and messages being piped into the homes of the drones were properly engineered. All agreed that there was a need for better entertainment to keep the drones occupied.

When we look across time at American society and observe the drones dancing in the all-seeing eye of the consoles as though they were puppets on a string or sticklike figures drawn on the walls of a cave and miraculously brought to life by "animators" to negotiate an obstacle course of no trespassing signs and arrive at "retail outlets" with their coupons and credit cards to stock up on designer jeans and wide-screen TVs as though they were themselves "players" in one of those ingenious games devised by the consoles to occupy the drones, we must pause again and wonder how so many millions were lured out of their homes each day to serve this system, whether as consumers or as "personnel." The engagement of the latter in superfluous activities as a condition for remaining alive, the sole purpose of which was to enrich the consoles, and the engagement of the former in superfluous "shopping," the sole purpose of which was also to enrich the consoles, was coordinated with such skill that wherever the consumer drone turned a service drone was on hand to serve him, each of the latter faithfully arriving at his station every day at the appointed hour utilizing complex transportation systems while commodities were put in place by delivery systems no less complex and even entailing the enlistment of child labor in distant regions of the globe. In our society, of course, "production" and "consumption" cancel one another out in accordance with the General Law of Economic Redundancy, making them marginal activities and leaving us free to engage in higher pursuits while the Central Unit sees to our basic needs. Consequently, we are happy, while the Earth creatures, as far as can be understood from their own testimony, were not, when all is said and done.

The "happiness" of the Earth creatures must be assessed at two levels, that of the drones and that of the consoles. The unhappiness of the drone was assured by the feeling implanted in him that whatever he had was not enough and thus he was "motivated" always to want more. This of course was a ploy utilized by the consoles to keep the drone strapped into the system and always striving for unattainable ends, like a rat on a treadmill. The small rewards given to the rat or drone keep him going while the "output" of this unfortunate creature is harnessed by the console to move mountains for his own ends. At a certain point, as we have mentioned, the drone "takes stock" and realizes that he isn't getting anywhere. The question is to what extent this feeling is offset by those same small rewards that keep him going. It must be said again that for the most part a balance is struck and the ordinary drone seesaws between a state of mild depression as he contemplates his sorry condition and a state of mild elation as he contemplates the next hamburger. Often, however, he is at odds with the female drone who shares his quarters, which can be seen from the fact that so many decouple despite the inducements of sex, financial security and the maintenance of a "home." Often he is also at odds with his "children," whose identity has not been established with certainty but are presumably the small-size drones who join the full-grown male and female at the breakfast table for Sugar Puffs before the "family" disperses to perform its assigned tasks. These tasks, as we have indicated, are generally unrewarding, a kind of drudgery that turns the drone into a moving part in a giant machine. Understandably he is often out of sorts and has to unwind with a couple of beers at the end of the day, occasionally breaking a bottle over someone's head.

The consoles, on the other hand, have every reason to be happy. It is true that we can never observe them directly, as they use "actors" as stand-ins, and thus we must "read between the lines" to get an idea of their private lives, or rely on the "reports" of journalists, which in keeping with their limited ability are little more than strings of platitudes arranged in quasi-grammatical sequence by "editors." Nonetheless a picture emerges that seems to indicate that they too were not particularly happy, being like the drones at odds with their "wives," their "children" and one another. Did they too feel that whatever they had was not enough? Did they come to believe their own messages? Did they wish to become drone-like "heroes" in the morality tales that they themselves invented?

It has been argued that the malaise of drone and console alike derives not so much from his circumstances as from his condition. Uncontrollable forces move him and death annihilates him. Against these forces and against the horizon of death he tries to assert himself as an autonomous being. He tries to nurture a flattering idea of himself. He tries to affirm his essential worth but can only achieve a relative position among other claimants to "the sweet fruition of an earthly crown." He broods, he postures, he wallows in self-pity. Perhaps this is the reason he talks so much.

We have already spoken of the manner in which the drone began his day, over a cup of "coffee" and breakfast cereals. Apparently the male and female interfaced during the night, quite noisily, the female donning alluring bedclothes that exposed her long, bare legs and the male inserting a small, sausage-like appendage into her port after pinning her on the bed. Often, if we can judge from the morality tales on view in the all-seeing eye of the consoles, the drones engaged in "horseplay," chaining one another to the bedposts or "saddling up" and assuming an unorthodox position familiar to us from the monkeys, who conceivably adopted this method of interfacing after observing the drones. Interfacing generally left the drones exhausted and they proceeded to drop off to sleep. During this "sleep" they often "dreamt." The content of their "dreams" is known to us from various texts and apparently reveals their greatest anxieties in an incoherent manner, the brunt of them being more than they can bear. This manner of repression or sublimation carries over into their everyday lives as a tactic for avoiding whatever is unpleasant and maintaining a high opinion of themselves. Dreams are generally forgotten the moment the drone awakens as a further precaution. The drone then brushes his teeth and evacuates bodily wastes. After "breakfast" the family disperses. The male "goes to work." The female goes "shopping." The little ones go to "school." In this manner the entire family is drawn into the system and performs its appointed tasks.

We cannot say how the consoles spent the night or, as mentioned before, how they interfaced. Apparently they only renewed their activities in the morning when they issued new instructions through their "mouthpieces," generally prominent drones. What the consoles were doing while these "mouthpieces" were haranguing and cajoling the drones, other than observing them, we do not know. Perhaps it was at this time that they interfaced, in the privacy of their inner chambers. Perhaps they consulted among themselves and devised their stratagems. Perhaps they merely idled away their time in slothful repose eating bonbons.

Once outside the home, on his way to "work," the male drone often purchases a newspaper where the screaming headlines compete for his attention. When his attention is captured his eye rests for a moment on the rows of words, storing the more striking or agreeable ones in his "memory," where they will be added to his store of knowledge or repertoire of opinions. If the striking or agreeable words contradict previously memorized words he will discard one or the other in accordance with his biases. Then he will move on to the sports page.

At the same hour the female drone makes a beeline for the "shopping center," the "adrenaline" already flowing. She has, perhaps, a list, or a fistful of ads or coupons torn out of a newspaper. The shock of seeing so many other drones overwhelms her for a moment but she gets her bearings quickly enough and feels a kind of elation as she plunges into the crowd. The thought of examining new lines of products, juicers and pitters and grinders and timers and crushers and poppers and slicers and mixers, not to mention perfumes and deodorants and creams and jellies and lotions, sets off various "programs" in her brain that take her to the appropriate "outlet." Once there a feeling of calm settles over her. She is "inside." Everything is within reach. She browses. She savors the atmosphere. She takes out her checkbook or credit card.

The "little ones" arrive at "school," going to their assigned "places" like little soldiers. A female wearing her hair in a bun calls them to attention and "teaches" for the next five or six hours. The "little ones" fidget, cough, sneeze, giggle, belch, make faces, pick their noses, deface their desks, scrape their feet, scratch their behinds and pass notes. The "teacher" becomes "cross" and "punishes" the most blatant offenders, making them stand in a corner or sit outside the principal's office. Sometimes she is surprised when one of them tries to stick a knife in her stomach.

The male drone arrives at "work" and removes his hat and coat. He is foreman of a plant manufacturing dog food. He is assistant director of sales for a company selling vacation homes in Dubai.

He is chief bookkeeper of a firm marketing bowling balls. He cleans swimming pools, he fries burgers, he tightens screws. He has coffee and a donut and gazes at his female coworkers for a while entertaining vague notions of interfacing with them. He engages in imaginary conversations with various adversaries and nemeses, and sometimes with his "wife," who often falls into the same category. He daydreams, he doodles, he shilly-shallies. At five o'clock he punches out.

The female drone meets her friends for lunch and they talk about their husbands' affairs, or their own. They also talk about the trouble they're having with the "little ones" and their plans for refurnishing their homes and what they bought that day. Afterwards they take in a matinee. Their phones ring constantly, now the children, now the husbands, now the lovers, and some shopkeeper about a check that bounced. By the time the female gets home she's exhausted. It's been a long day.

In the evening everyone gathers around the console to receive further instructions. The console— as always, we presume—observes them with a measure of amusement, and certainly with satisfaction. The drones can always be counted on to carry out their appointed tasks and assemble in the evening in the "living" room, where the console presides. Not having had them there for most of the day he has a great deal to say: first a news update cataloguing the death toll in the last few hours to capture their attention, then a sitcom to put them in a good mood and a few "commercial messages" telling them what to eat for dinner; during dinner a game show to remind them that there are big prizes out there to be won by the lucky few; after that, the serious stuff—prime time action and suspense, hospitals, prisons, police precincts, private investigators, high-priced lawyers, and then a late night talk show to wind things down.

So one day ends and another begins and the drones work and shop and receive their instructions and have their ups and downs and apparently "die" at a certain point, hoping for a better life in the Hereafter.

Money continues to change hands and the wars go on. The consoles congratulate one another on a job well done.

On the disks that we have recovered every inch of space in the all-seeing eye of the consoles is filled with drones acting as stand-ins or mouthpieces for the consoles or in their own names. We see great swarms of them as thick as locusts and looking very much alike so that it is only with great difficulty that we are able to make the distinctions that enable us to understand their way of life and the subtle means by which they are controlled as well as the nature of the consoles who stood at the pinnacle of this society. To the untrained eye the movement of the drones might seem chaotic, and yet nothing occurs that is not planned and guided, unless in those regions of the planet where the consoles are not fully in control. The greater their control the greater the regimentation of the society and the greater the illusion of freedom. The console does not rule with a whip but through the creation of frameworks and channels that lead the drone in the desired direction without his being aware of being led. As control grows tighter the frameworks seem to expand and the channels to multiply whereas in fact they have only become more elaborate like a spider's web in order to enmesh the drone even further. In the end there was no escape from the system.

While it is generally agreed that the lifespan of the consoles was just eight years, it is not known how long the drones lived. Conceivably they lived longer than the consoles as an enormous investment was made to instill in them the values and patterns of behavior that were beneficial to the consoles and it was therefore in the best interests of the latter to have such docile and well-trained creatures around for as long as possible. To this end they were filled with medicinal drugs to offset the ill effects of the "processed" foodstuffs they were encouraged to ingest and cosmetically enhanced to deceive them into believing they were young and healthy. All this effort notwithstanding, the drones nonetheless seem to have dragged themselves around with considerable excess baggage, being, in the euphemism of the day, intestinally challenged. Some of them couldn't get through a door.

In contrast to the fat drones, who took on the aspect of gelatinous slugs, the consoles grew sleeker and more streamlined with the passage of time. Apparently their cognitive faculties were upgraded as well. This "parting of the ways" between the drones and the consoles conceivably marks the turning point in our own evolution. The drones were doomed and apparently became extinct first, wallowing in their own fat as they consumed the "snacks" offered to them by the consoles in their daily sessions before the all-seeing eye, moved like zombies as they performed the tasks assigned to them and repeated the opinions taught to them, stood in lines and sat in waiting rooms, obeyed the rules, followed procedures, learned the ropes, called things by their proper names, filled out the forms, dialed the numbers, submitted their requests, appeared at the appointed hours, punched the clocks, exchanged pleasantries, paid their fees and dues, and blinked stupidly at the all-seeing eye as they absorbed the thousands of messages being rained down on their heads.

In the course of time the consoles must have discovered that they could do without the drones, conducting their wars in virtual space and in effect living entirely inside themselves until something resembling our own Central Unit evolved and they were able to abandon the dying planet that had given birth to them. Long before that time American civilization had also ended. The old order was forgotten, the old texts were buried in the ground, and new empires were founded. Such is the course of history, and as sure as we are standing here today a time will come when we too will be a distant memory.

FROM THE MINUTES OF THE 458,734TH MEETING OF THE INTERGALACTIC EXPLORATION SOCIETY

At our last session we spoke in very general terms of the creatures who inhabited the dead planet called Earth 500,000 years ago. Our aim was to describe the social climate that prevailed there, particularly in the region known as the United States of America, which, owing to the peculiarities of its doomed society, throws everything pertaining to that planet into bold relief and makes it easier to understand why the civilization of the Earth came to an end. We noted that there were two forms of intelligent life there, designated Console I and Console II, the latter prevailing after a period of apparent coexistence, and a race of drones who served them, enslaved as a kind of domestic animal and organized into a hierarchy of "orders." These can be identified in the texts under their "medieval" nomenclatures, namely, "talkers" (*oratores*), "entertainers" (*stultores*), "businessmen" (*mercatores et negotiatores*), "warriors" (*bellatores*) and "workers" (*laboratores*). Each order was exploited by the consoles to further their aims and rewarded in accordance with a system that cannot be rationally explained at this point.

The talkers and the *stultores* were the "aristocracy" of drone society, the *mercatores* clearly a kind of "middle class," with the exception of a small number of well-connected *negotiatores*, and the *bellatores* and *laboratores* the unfortunate "lower" class, though hardly more unfortunate than the members of the middle class in that the latter were controlled no less strictly than the former, albeit with a few more rewards thrown in "to sweeten the pot."

The elevation of a drone from one order to

another, though infrequent, was highly publicized, with the aim of creating the illusion that all drones could advance in this way. To foster this illusion, and keep the drones "glued to their seats," occasional competitions were organized in which a worker drone was chosen by "judges" to become an entertainer after demonstrating his ability to "sing songs." The judges were generally *stultores* who had become "talkers." Occasionally ordinary drones were allowed to vote for their favorite *stultor*, in much the same way as they voted for the producer consoles who would control them. The results of these competitions were announced with great fanfare after the general drone population was reminded to imbibe their pacifying beverages, lest their excitement exceed acceptable bounds. Worker drones could also be elevated in this manner and become stultors by demonstrating their prowess at hitting a ball with a stick or pretending to be a hero in the various "morality tales" worked up by the consoles to instruct the drones.

Though it is not clear how and when the consoles established their primacy, it is in fact possible to reconstruct the history of the United States of America, however tentatively, through closer examination of these very same "morality tales," so prominently featured on the memory disks we have uncovered. While the aim of these tales was to instruct and pacify the drones, they incidentally offer fascinating glimpses into the origins of this society and its unspoken assumptions. Though genres vary, the central themes remain the same, most often depicting the triumph of the "hero," which allows the drone to live vicariously through a surrogate self and forget his sorry condition for a while. In these tales we are also able to observe the drone in various geographical and temporal settings and in his daily occupations. One of these settings is generally referred to as the Wild West and clearly belongs to a relatively early time when land was still being "grabbed" and the consoles were apparently just beginning the process of expropriating the country's resources. This is a "pre-industrial" age where drones were allotted "homesteads" that the consoles often stole from them. Sometimes the "hero" was a sheriff or marshal with a colorful "sidekick." Sometimes the sheriff or marshal was a villain himself, "in cahoots" with the land-grabber, in which case he would not have a colorful sidekick. The "hero" might then be a "stranger" or "loner" with a mysterious past. He would inevitably fall in love with the beautiful and virginal daughter of one of the homesteaders, or perhaps with a buxom "widow" struggling to keep her farm going, in which case it would be made clear that the said widow had not interfaced in quite some time, so that for all practical purposes she could also be thought of as virginal, or at least starved for sex, which the hero would provide after a decent interval. It can easily be imagined how satisfying these spectacles must have been for the drones clustered around the consoles watching them and enjoying the snacks they had been instructed to purchase. The "hero" would also be depicted as not having interfaced for a while, if at all, being "pure" or bashful or nursing some terrible wound, his wife murdered by "Injuns" or even by the cronies of the villainous sheriff or marshal who did not have a colorful sidekick. In the ensuing land war the land-grabber would at first have the upper hand. The hero might then sign on as a farmhand, being remote but respectful toward the virgin's father or the widow's uncle, always addressing his elders as "sir" and thereby establishing his credentials as someone who subscribed to cherished American values and was therefore worthy of being a hero. In the climactic shootout the hero would take on the land-grabber's "gang," who would be depicted falling off roofs and crashing through windows. The villainous land-grabber would be the last to get his, perhaps taking the virgin or widow hostage, perhaps handling her inappropriately to stimulate the sexual appetite of the drones gathered around the consoles with their mouths hanging open, which stimulation was most often achieved by allowing the drones to catch a glimpse of her long, bare leg or plump breast as she struggled against the villain, at which point the hero would put a bullet through his head.

The myth of the hero was clearly the great myth of American life. The moral rectitude and sexual purity of the classic hero were ideals "whitewashing" the moral baseness and sexual impurity of the common drone. The solitariness and self-reliance of the classic hero embodied the drone's dream of freedom from the controls of society. The terrible wound that the hero often bore in his breast fed the drone's fantasies of healing love. The triumph of the hero against console-like types reflected the drone's resentment of his "betters."

However, not all heroes were perfect. Within these morality tales a "modern" hero evolved who was seldom pure and often morally flawed. He was a tough cop whose wife had left him because he drank too much. He was a former commando who had been booted out of Special Forces for disobeying orders and causing the death of his best friend. He drank too much because his partner had been shot while the hero was sleeping with some stripper or even shaking down a drug dealer. He disobeyed orders because his commanding officer was corrupt or a coward. Back on the street he hooks up with a tough broad who is trying to get out from under the thumb of a mobster, or maybe with an innocent midwestern type trying to find out how her brother was killed in the big city, or maybe with his best friend's widow, or maybe with his own estranged wife. The flawed hero is morally more like the drone and more vocal in his resentment of authority, so the identification is stronger. He is the kind of redeemed hero the drone would like to be. In the end he wreaks havoc, just as the drone would like to do, and gets to interface with the tough broad or the midwestern type or his friend's widow or his own wife, making a fresh start.

The production of morality tales and other forms of entertainment comprised an industry no less important to the American economy than the production of acidic beverages and "processed" foods. Though no one would have missed or desired the products of these industries had they not been habituated to them, their existence was essential, for the American economy would have collapsed without them, forcing Americans to go back to an earlier time when "consumers" ate healthy foods and entertained themselves. This would have put a big hole in the pockets of the consoles, so their leaders arranged generous tax cuts and other incentives to enable them to produce more unnecessary commodities and employ more drones at the minimum wage.

Some have claimed that the pictures produced for the "viewing enjoyment" of the drones in the all-seeing eye of the consoles do not reflect reality, that the "actors" neither speak nor act like actual drones, let alone like consoles, that the dramas invented by the producers do not represent the actual conditions of life in America and that the "reports" presented by solemn "reporters" are distorted and superficial versions of undigested events. In this respect it may be noted parenthetically that the failure of reporters to report accurately and meaningfully is not necessarily a result of bad intentions. Most often it is a result of lack of talent, for if they could see deeper or write better they would not be reporters, they would be historians and even novelists. As for the actors and producers associated with the morality tales presented to the drones, we have already noted the mythological nature of these extravaganzas and should therefore not expect to find in them a literal reflection of reality but rather a guide to the "dreams" of the audience to which they are addressed.

The drone, as we have suggested, was ignorant, that is, totally dependent on "reporters," "analysts," and talk show "experts" for his understanding of the world around him. He could not read anything longer than a column or two of newsprint. He could not find his own country on an unmarked map. He could not describe at any length the most important events of his own history or explain the most elementary scientific principles or speak intelligently about the cultural achievements of his race. However, it cannot be said that keeping the drones ignorant was an express aim of the consoles, though there were of course a great many things that the consoles did not wish the drones to know. On the contrary, wishing to inculcate values beneficial to themselves and prepare the drones to serve them, the consoles organized an "educational" system for this very purpose and certainly would have been surprised when it turned out that the drones learned very little within this system and indeed developed a strong aversion to learning as such as a result of being put through it. This was in marked contrast to the ease with which messages and instructions were absorbed when shown in the all-seeing eye of the consoles, though of course this entailed endless repetition, which in itself was not very different from the methods employed by the "schools." Yet in one case the drones, and particularly the young, sat transfixed and did precisely what they were told to do while in the other they fidgeted and couldn't even get their multiplication table straight.

Clearly the writers of messages and instructions were more sophisticated than the "educators." We cannot say why one type of console was drawn to "education" and another to message writing. We can only speculate about the failure of the educator to educate when he had before him the successful model of the message writer. Our own researchers have indeed detected a fatal flaw in the methodology of these ancient educators. For unlike the message writers, who recognized and were able to exploit the passivity of the drone, not to mention his unconscious drives, the educators only recognized what they regarded as the "evil" in him and therefore concluded, inappropriately, that the drone must be forced to do what is "good," in this case to learn, an attitude that derives directly from the primitive religion of these creatures. The young drone was thus made to sit perfectly still and ingest huge volumes of "material," memorize it and repeat it. The immediate effect of this bludgeon-like method was to destroy the innate curiosity of the drone and transform him from a creature who wanted to know everything into a creature who wanted to know nothing, except for a scholarly few whose ability and ambition could not be destroyed by the system and therefore survived it.

The consoles thus exploited the laziness and passivity of the drone to fill his head with artfully designed messages and instructions while the educator overwhelmed him with information that bored him to death instead of devising methods that captured his attention. Thus the drones were "shortchanged," being made to "pay" for an education they did not receive and becoming easy marks for reporters and analysts who were only slightly less ignorant than themselves, seldom even understanding the languages of the countries they reported from or commented on.

The consoles are said to have arrived in America from a foreign shore, at some indeterminate date. We do not know if they brought the drones with them or found them already there on the new continent. Proponents of the latter view identify the drones with the so-called "Injuns" who are occasionally observed in the morality tales on view in the all-seeing eye of the consoles. However, it is more likely that the drones and "Injuns" were rivals, for they are often viewed destroying one another, though it may be assumed that the consoles had a hand in this. In any case, we do not know of a time when the consoles were without drones to serve them. From the outset the consoles asserted themselves, "grabbing," as we have said, whatever they laid their eyes on and soon establishing their hegemony, though formally they were ruled by a "king" who sat in a distant place, across the great sea. When the said king interfered with Commerce, well-heeled Americans "rebelled," instructing the drones to do the same, which they eagerly did. Everyone "took up arms," and apparently did not put them down until their civilization was itself destroyed.

It is in this context that we first encounter George Washington Bush, though it is not known precisely when he came to prominence. What is known is that at a certain point America declared its "independence" and produced a Constitution establishing the property rights of the consoles and the means by which they would maintain power and control the drone population. The consoles then seated themselves in various "houses" and assemblies and proceeded to oversee a system that maintained the existing inequalities. These "houses" were often magnificent edifices built to accommodate the rather squat figures of the console "representatives," who held forth at great length and enacted laws in such profusion that only trained "lawyers" could keep track of them and these lawyers incessantly argued among themselves about the meaning of these laws which even the legislators did not fully understand so that "judges" were often required to intervene while the poor drones sat hat in hand waiting for their fate to be decided. Naturally enough, since these laws were made by the country's most powerful individuals, they were most lenient in regard to their own crimes and most severe in regard to the crimes of others. Thus the powerful permitted themselves to "grab" as much land as they wished but punished mercilessly those unfortunate creatures led by circumstance to "grab" a loaf of bread.

In the eight years of his life, before being recycled, George Washington Bush doggedly enforced the laws of this land and conducted its wars, transferring "money" from the poor to the rich and taking care of his good friends the Havemores, a family that apparently had close ties with his own. Frequently he took long vacations on his plantation with his wife, Martha, where he liked to ride and shoot. Occasionally he made a brief visit to the troops and assured them that one way or another his wars were going to be won, neglecting to tell them by whom.

The Havemores had probably arrived in America together with the Bushes, soon carving out little empires for themselves and sticking up thousands of signs saying keep out private property trespassers will be shot on sight or failing that prosecuted to the full extent of the law. They also got fat government contracts and big tax writeoffs. They ate well and had black maids and Spanish-speaking gardeners. Money wasn't a problem. Dick Havemore was fixed up with a little board chairmanship between stints as a public "servant." That netted him millions. Ditto for Don Havemore.

In managing American society, the dilemma of the consoles was clear: by instructing the drones, among other things, to consume "foodstuffs" that would ultimately kill them they were in effect "cutting off the branch" they were sitting on, much like skydiving instructors who knowingly supply their students with defective parachutes. However, this does not seem to have disturbed them in the least, as the "little ones" soon enough replaced the "senior citizens" as eager and pliant consumers, so that a kind of natural cycle was established and no carcinogen-bearing "chow" or fat-saturated "grub" went uneaten, even by the toothless. The producers of these harmful substances were apparently connected in some way with the ubiquitous Havemore family and therefore received certain privileges denied to other "pushers." Ditto for polluters of the air and poisoners of the soil.

Some researchers have claimed that the drones were subjected to a special surgical procedure in infancy to remove part of their brain and ensure their docility, much like the "neutering" of domestic animals. Though this did not prevent the frequent outbursts of violence among these creatures it ensured their receptivity to messages and instructions, making it nearly impossible for them to form thoughts outside the system of concepts to which they were trained to respond. With a complete brain, it is argued, the drones would immediately have "seen through" the messages they received just as they saw through "glass" and understood clearly what was hidden on the other side. This is merely a supposition, and as we have found no evidence to support such an argument we are inclined to look elsewhere for an explanation of this phenomenon. In fact there is a school of thought that maintains that the drones did understand the deceptive nature of the messages they received and yet were still compelled to respond to them, which perhaps indicates elements inherent in their "psychological" or even biological makeup that caused them to "buckle under," like sheep being led to the slaughter. In the "animal kingdom" such herd instincts along with the primacy of dominant males generally ensured the health and prosperity of the species but among the drones these same instincts made them easy prey for the consoles as well as for their own kind. Not only "weak" individuals were weeded out to preserve the vigor of the herd, but in fact *most* individuals were weeded out, becoming true drones in the service of the strong, whose polished language mesmerized them like the language of "commercial messages," though, as we have noted, they were more than likely able to "see through" these messages. In the latter case the message writer addressed the subconscious of the drone and thereby animated drives and forces that the drone could not control while in the former case the strong merely asserted their authority and exploited the primitive need of the drone to follow a leader.

At the same time, as mentioned, the consoles encouraged the drones to affirm the values that served their own interests, such as patriotism to ensure that they would be prepared to fight in the wars organized by the consoles, free enterprise to ensure that the consoles would not be hindered in their rapacious pursuit of wealth, democracy to ensure that the vast majority of Americans who lost the big races would be "good sports" about it and accept the dominance of the few, and of course "hard work," "tenacity," "honesty," "decency," "modesty" and "respect for authority" to ensure that they would keep their noses to the grindstone. So successful were the consoles in inculcating these values that the drones who suffered the most in this system invoked them as evidence of the superiority of the American way of life, unless they were color-coded black and consequently not really privy to the American way of life, despite the frequent casting of blacks as judges and police captains in the morality tales, which was conceivably a subtle counterweight to the black criminals in these tales as much as a gratuitous crumb tossed to the disinherited.

Many of the drones used to transmit commercial messages seem to have been trained as ventriloquists, utilizing a variety of "voices" to encourage ordinary drones to acquire commodities. Sometimes they spoke "sincerely," sometimes enthusiastically, sometimes even "humorously" to endear themselves to the drone family gathered around the console by pretending not to take the commodity seriously. Clearly a great deal of thought was invested in the selection of these voices and the elaboration of the little dramas played out in the all-seeing eye of the consoles in order to get around the natural defenses of the drone and lead him by the nose, though the fact that huge sums of "money" seem to have been invested in this endeavor leads us to believe that the consoles were confident of a positive result, counting on the stupidity of the drone to ensure his ultimate acquiescence to whatever messages and instructions they transmitted. There is no question that they "studied" the drones quite closely and therefore understood their weaknesses, which they cynically exploited in order to enrich themselves, feeling, we imagine, considerable contempt for creatures who were taken in so easily and perhaps making a few "jokes" at their expense as they sat around the office dreaming up new messages. We can also understand the enormous satisfaction such consoles must have experienced in getting tens of millions of drones to memorize and even repeat their inane slogans and jingles. The commercial message, together with the three-minute video clip, seems to have been the great art form of late American civilization, superseding literature, painting, sculpture and classical music and clearly tailored to the waning attention span of the drone.

In addition to appearing in the "news" broadcasts, most often as criminals or victims, ordinary drones also appeared occasionally on the "talk shows" alongside the experts and analysts to complain about their misery or display a certain quality of freakishness which the experts and analysts might then discuss in a learned manner. Freakishness and misery were also the leading motifs in the confessional or confrontational shows in which a "host" egged on the guests until a fistfight broke out. These were rare opportunities for the drones to "have their day" and get an all expenses paid trip to Hollywood or New York in the bargain. Granted these drones were generally "bellatores" and "laboratores," and as such didn't count for much, but as they comprised at least a third of the American population there were plenty of them around, so producers had little trouble finding large numbers who were freakish or miserable enough to appear on daytime and even prime time TV. The freakish and the miserable were also brought into the competitions to give the "studio audience" and viewers at home a good laugh before getting down to the serious business of upgrading a worker drone into an entertainment drone. The criminals among them had their own day on "cop" shows and were usually last seen with their faces in the gutter and their hands cuffed behind their backs.

Many of these criminals were housed in "prisons," which were sometimes the subject of the morality tales, as were law courts and hospitals, and if the confrontations in these tales were less convincing than the "live" confrontations in the "reality" shows, they at least had the advantage of being bloodier and were therefore suitable vehicles for peddling sanitary products and pain killers. Though many of the drones were squeamish, the thirst for blood among them was always present in varying degrees and therefore the producers of sanitary products and pain killers made sure they got plenty of it and deliberated solemnly about which of the bloodbaths would "move" their products more quickly. Mr. Bush was proud to be associated with such producers, the producers of bloodbaths and the producers of sanitary products, and assured the drones that they helped make America great, like the Havemores.

Other nations tried to imitate the American way of life, but with less success, being perhaps less "materialistic" or having less stupid populations. The Europeans, for example, had historically never found it necessary to foster the illusion that their "orders" were fluid and that anyone could improve his lot through ambition and hard work. Everyone knew his place and consequently there were fewer disappointments and fewer mental breakdowns. The illusion of freedom and social or economic mobility left tens of millions of "middling" Americans with the uncomfortable feeling that they had no one to blame but themselves for their lack of success. Some therefore pretended to be successful, "aping" the manner of prominent drones, reading book reviews instead of books and filling their homes with fake antiques. Some just talked big. The poor, on the other hand, knew better and understandably became bitter. Nonetheless, in the latter part of the 20th century, many Europeans became infected by the democratic "bug" and began to dream of prominence in the American tradition, becoming easy prey for the European consoles who let loose hosts of reporters, message writers, experts and analysts to control and manipulate them.

All this being said, we cannot deny the possibility that we are "misreading" the materials at hand. Certain scholars have argued that it is inconceivable that a society should function in the manner that the United States of America seems to have functioned, that "leaders" should engage in such flagrant deceptions and communicate in a language consisting substantially of meaningless rhetorical devices, that wealth should be hoarded by the few, and that the many should consent to and even celebrate a system that strangles them. We too acknowledged that the images projected in the all-seeing eye of the consoles often had hidden meanings, so that while the "news" broadcasts were distorted narratives and the "talk shows" were forums for idle chatter, the morality tales were mostly parables. We believed that we perceived a purpose in these spectacles and the messages that accompanied them, which were designed to control and manipulate the drones. And yet at the same time we found it difficult to understand how the drones could be so stupid as to be taken in by them and organize their lives precisely in accordance with the instructions they received from the consoles. Accordingly, we concluded that certain "psychological" and even biological factors must be at work making the drones such easy prey. Many of these factors were apparently "selected out" in the monkeys who succeeded the drones and conceivably form the "link" between the drones and the consoles. It is also conceivable that the consoles themselves are linked in some way to us, though if this is the case there have obviously been many significant intermediate stages in the evolutionary process.

This is the most reasonable interpretation of the materials at hand. However, certain other interpretations have been put forward which it may be profitable to examine. One is that it was the drones who originally were the masters of the consoles and became their slaves in a "coup" of some kind, or perhaps through some insidious process in which the positions of slave and master were reversed without the drones fully understanding what had occurred. Proponents of this view argue that this reversal of positions must have occurred in a very early stage of their common history because it is inconceivable that drones would have subjected their own kind to the atrocities commonplace in this society and conspired to cheat, starve and poison their brethren, stepping over bodies, as it were, in pursuit of their own ends. Only creatures of another species, it is argued, would be capable of such "inhumanity."

This is a compelling argument, but the fact is we see many prominent drones behaving no less callously than the consoles, such as "reporters" in pursuit of "stories" or "mercatores" and "negotiatores" in pursuit of "money." In essence there is no great difference between the behavior of drones and consoles aside from the fact that the consoles are smarter and more powerful. Nor are we convinced that a "rebellion" of the kind described took place. It seems far more likely that the consoles were the masters of the drones from the moment these two species came into contact with one another, though we concede that there may have been a time when the drones ruled themselves, in a society not much different in principle, if far less sophisticated and far less vicious, from the one organized by the consoles as soon as they established their dominance, or were perhaps ruled by the monkeys until the consoles came along. In the latter case it is also doubtful if the cruelty that characterized relations between master and slave would have been so marked, despite the natural aggressiveness of the monkey. The mind of the monkey ran along less fiendish lines and he certainly would not have known how to run a whorehouse or an advertising agency.

Though we are inclined to believe that the consoles ruled the drones from the outset, we acknowledge that the entrenchment of this rule may have occurred over a certain period of time during which the consoles devised ever more sophisticated methods with which to enslave the drones. However, as we can see from what we believe to be early disks belonging to Console I, their methods were quite sophisticated to begin with and the drones sat at the feet of the consoles with the same rapt attention as they displayed in a later period, consuming the same acidic beverages and breakfast cereals and no doubt dreaming the same dreams of acquiring commodities, pinning females on the ground and destroying other drones in the name of freedom and democracy. The only significant differences seem to have been in the depiction of the way drones interfaced and in the system of color coding. With respect to color coding the early disks restrict themselves to a simple "black and white" differentiation while later disks display a greater variety of "colored" drones in positions of prominence, like the judges and police captains mentioned above and even an occasional brain surgeon or nuclear physicist. With respect to interfacing the early disks rarely displayed females with long, bare legs or any other provocatively exposed body parts, unless they were "beauty queens" in "swimsuits" or "ladies" in handsome gowns that showed some "cleavage," or perhaps "loose women" flaunting their wares or innocent "girls" bathing in the nude and offering a tantalizing glimpse of their rosy flesh or well-endowed females being seized and pinned on the ground, or anything else the producers could get away with to excite the drones and capture their attention. The later disks are less coy and undoubtedly lost some of their effect, forcing the producers to go to greater lengths "to get a rise" out of the jaded drone though of course without offending "public taste."

The system of seemingly flexible boundaries that in fact enclosed a series of rigidly constructed boxes "channeling" the movement of the drones from one prison to the other—from the home to the school, from the workplace to the mall, and finally to the grave—with numerous "side-trips" on circular byways that led back to their starting point, comprised the whole of drone society. The few who rebelled against it became outcasts or outlaws, deprived of its meager material rewards and the comfort of the herd. They gathered "on the other side," in an undefined space, beyond the reach of the messages and instructions that rained down on the heads of the drones from morning to night, and consequently ruled themselves. The consoles despised them, persecuted them, tempted them, or simply ignored them, pretending they didn't exist. The drones, for their part, feared them, thinking they would shatter the illusions on which their peace of mind was based and divert the thoughts of the "little ones" from the games and snacks that nurtured them. Such rebels were called "beatniks" and "hippies" by some and sociopaths by others. Fortunately the former generally "grew up" and recanted while the latter generally ended up in prison. In this way American society was able to endure for a while longer, until the final catastrophe that ended human civilization, paving the way for more rational beings like ourselves.

ANOTHER KIND OF HARMONY

In the red room the figures come and go. In the red light they give off an eerie glow. In the red dust they twist and turn. There is nothing but this: the red light and the figures that come and go. There are no walls in the red room. It is as big as you want it to be. No one can say for certain how their history began. They are like us but not like us. They float through the air, greeting each other cordially in their peregrinations. It is like groping in the dark. Everything is steeped in shadow, dark and red. Who comes? Is it male or female, friend or foe? They float toward us. They veer to the right or to the left. Everything flows. You cannot see them but they are there.

They are intelligent creatures, that much is certain—more intelligent than we will ever be. They communicate as if by magic. They reproduce unwittingly. They do not understand death. Otherwise they are pretty much like us. They laugh and cry. They socialize. They enjoy a good meal.

John and Mary were a couple. They'd known each other since they were kids so naturally enough they stuck together when the time came for the big migration. They drifted south with the others in the laborious way such creatures have, through the red shadows and heavy mist. In truth they thought the world of one another. John saw Mary in the most flattering light, as though she were an angel. Everything about her was perfect in his eyes. Mary thought John was the handsomest creature she had ever seen and would provide for all her needs. He would maintain her and protect her and embrace her before they slept.

They all hovered in the red air until everyone

was there and then settled in. John and Mary rented a lovely house, a split level affair with an arbor out back and shopping nearby. John worked at the Information Center. It was either that or the drudgery of a recycling plant with the attendant risk of being recycled oneself. Mary took care of the house. You wouldn't have thought there'd be much to do there but between the shopping and cleaning and preparing meals she was exhausted at the end of the day and John often had to recharge her when he got home. That was sometimes a problem because the weaker she got the less of her he could see. "Let's get some color back in your cheeks," was their standing joke. At the Information Center John processed data, running them through his PS or Personal System (PS) and saving whatever was interesting for private use, always passing it on to Mary when they interfaced so they had that as an additional bond and often chatted about arcane things, batting ideas back and forth, so they got a reputation as intellectual types in the neighborhood. Mary could handle whatever John threw at her, even though her PS was less sophisticated than his, being needed only for the household chores. Both of them had opted for the multitrack system, meaning they could be in many places at the same time. Therefore John was lodged permanently at the Center while always being at home and Mary could go anywhere she liked and still take care of the house. On the other hand, experts agreed that the multitrack system led to a high rate of decoupling as interfacing with more than one partner became a simple matter of being in the right place at the right time with no one the wiser for it unless the suspicious party got a detective to "bug" the guilty party's system. John and Mary, however, were faithful to one another, never having interfaced with anyone else, except of course for social or professional purposes.

Mary did wonderful things with the standard oil-based paste that was distributed every morning at the Food Center. She supplemented it with taste options and they imbibed the whole concoction through a straw. The Manufacturing Center was always coming out with new lines of straws and naturally enough they became conversation pieces and their designers were said to have become rich and powerful figures in the world of haute couture. Some of the straws cost a small fortune and John and Mary sometimes had arguments about how much she was putting out on them, as occasionally she tended to go overboard as in the case of a candy-striped model inlaid with precious stones that she couldn't resist at a holiday sale. "I'll stick to the old plexiform if it's all right with you," John said, and Mary was almost in tears and said she was going to bring it right back if that was how he felt about it and John of course relented and afterwards they interfaced as they hadn't interfaced for weeks.

Every six months they had to sign in at the Service Center for a general update and hardware check. This was a lengthy procedure and Mary always complained of headaches afterwards. On one such occasion, floating through the corridors in a disoriented state, she wandered into a storeroom for discarded parts and saw her old CPU there. It was a wrenching experience, bringing back memories she'd thought she'd lost, so she interfaced with it on the spot and came back home with a rosy glow. John asked her what had happened and she explained it to him and John said he'd heard about such things but pointed out that it was strongly condemned in certain quarters as a form of auto-degradation. Mary got angry and said, "You ought to try it first before you put it down," and they had another fight.

John and Mary usually spent their evenings at home relaxing in their networking box. Sometimes they had friends over and then Mary would whip up a quick paste and lay out their best straws. Their next-door neighbors had three kids, so small you could hardly see them. They were kept in a kind of pod, as was the fashion these days, interfacing freely until they fell asleep. Mary kept asking the neighbors all kinds of questions and John could see she wanted kids herself and even asked them how you got them but they didn't know. "One day they're just there," was what they said. Nobody seemed to know where the kids came from. It was a great mystery, one of the few mysteries still left in fact.

Kids demanded a lot of time and had to be interfaced from morning to night, which took a lot out of a parent. They also required special pastes. You could shut them down of course and stick them on a shelf, but what was the sense of having kids if that was what you were going to do with them?

The high point of the year was the recitation of the history of the race with its mythological beginnings. Nobody believed these myths but they were recited nonetheless and pulling your plug was a punishable offense. It was said that once there had been many forms of life but in the end the creatures of the red room had prevailed and now they were alone in a universe no larger than their own minds, a universe not so much reduced in size as reinvented to suit their requirements. The universe, their teachers liked to say, is in your heads, bigger or smaller as the case may be.

The wars of the creatures of the red room had lasted eons. At first they had enslaved all those whom they vanquished but they really had no need for them and besides even as slaves they competed for the precious paste that was the stuff of their lives and so the creatures of the red room had eliminated all the vanquished races of the land, sea and air. John and Mary knew only a perfect world with enough paste for everyone. Those who regulated the social order sat in the center of the room and sent out messages every day. Mary relied on John to process them and was satisfied to receive a short resume when they interfaced at night. The number of messages coming in was so enormous that those equipped with ordinary PSs sometimes had trouble sorting them. John knew everything. Even the neighbors came to him for information and advice.

However, even in a perfect world there were signs of discontent. Not everyone was satisfied with his PS and occasionally there were demonstrations about the quality of the paste. Some thought it was being watered down and funneled off to the advantage of certain privileged individuals who inhabited a rarefied atmosphere seldom visited by lesser creatures. Nothing had ever been proved, however. Besides which, processing messages kept everyone pretty busy. John told Mary he wasn't sure everyone was getting the same messages and this may well have been the way things were regulated, but again no one could prove it, the flow of information being so immense that you barely had a chance to breathe.

The minute size of the creatures of the red room did not prevent them from performing herculean tasks by coupling and bonding to form huge conglomerates capable of moving even mountains. They were of course aided by the ingenious machines devised by the mechanically inclined, machines that gave the impression of being the true rulers of the realm, but this was of course an illusion, for the machines were ruled by those who built them, as was everyone else.

As nothing began and nothing ended there were no questions about the beginning and end of things, only about what appeared to be a protracted middle. No one wondered where this middle went or where it came from. It was just there, forever. John and Mary sometimes wondered how they would fill so much time. Sometimes Mary even got depressed and pulled her plug in the middle of the day and then John would have to spend half the night recharging her. He took her to the Service Center and they spoke to a counselor but afterwards Mary wandered off and interfaced with her old CPU again. The counselor said she was suffering from fatigue and suggested they take a vacation together. John found a suitable program and in less time than it took light to travel they were on the beach under a parasol sipping drinks that didn't taste like any paste they'd ever had before. There was a floor show every night and someone called Happy Hal exercised the females in the morning while the males played games with a ball. One afternoon they went to see a professional match in the local arena. A number of males ran and jumped for three hours and everyone cheered. Mary thought John could be out there too but John told her it wasn't as easy as it looked and that was why males who ran and jumped were so greatly admired and got extra paste. When they got back to the room John deactivated Mary's moving parts and they interfaced in new positions. Mary said, "Wow!" and it looked like she was back to her old self again.

The day after they got back home they found half a dozen kids in the house. Mary was beside herself with joy and sent John to get a pod. That evening as they sat in their networking box John had occasion to reflect on how well his life had turned out. Here was Mary with her sleek chassis and flashing lights, just as alluring as when he'd first interfaced with her, and now the six little ones lapping up their paste like kittens, though nearly invisible. He had an interesting job and a well-appointed house. He was sleek himself. Others, less fortunate, showed signs of wear and tear and didn't seem to be having much fun. That was too bad. John refused to feel guilty. Anyone in the red room could be happy. It was up to them.

John and Mary fitted out the kids' room with all the accessories recommended by the Information Center. When they were about a year old they began to float. That made it easier to get around. There was a playground near the house where Mary often took them, meeting females like herself and spending many pleasant afternoons chatting with them about family matters like interfacing and paste-making. When the kids were a little older they were upgraded and the information began to flow. Sometimes John or Mary had to help them sort it out and sometimes the kids learned things that John or Mary didn't know. Besides which, they interfaced in strange ways that sometimes shocked their parents. "The times are changing," John said philosophically. And it was true. The kids were barely out of their pods and were already engaging in auto-degradation, not to mention the music they listened to from morning till night.

Though the creatures of the red room inhabited a murky space, everything was crystal clear to them, they saw what we cannot see and knew what we will never know. Their limbs were like tentacles interfacing as they floated through the crowded air or paused to rest and information flowed through their veins like a thick elixir. They saw what they saw and knew what they knew in the clearest images, deep inside themselves. It hardly mattered what the world was like outside.

John and Mary had a family now. They were like all the other creatures of the red room. They stuck together. After their semiannual hardware checks they always took the kids on a family outing, exploring the outer edges of the red room. There were some who said there was a door in the room that led to other rooms no less vast and undefined than the one they inhabited but none had found it though many searched. The door is in your minds, their teachers said. You will only find it within yourselves.

Some even said that these other worlds had a beginning and an end, but the creatures of the red room could not grasp such a concept. If there was a beginning, what came before it, they asked; if there was an end, what came after it. No one could say. John and Mary could not remember a time when they had not been and could not imagine a time when they would not be. At the very worst you traded in your CPU, as in Mary's case when she'd had that virus that nearly erased her memory.

John got a promotion at the Information Center. Mary was having trouble with her chassis and had to be serviced twice a week until the problem cleared up. Fortunately she had a good sense of humor so whenever she wanted to interface she would say to John, "I need to be serviced, baby, and I mean now!" John had a good sense of humor too and would always reply, "Full service or self-service, ma'am?" This was of course "bedroom talk" and they always had a great deal of fun in bed, playing with each other's controls until their circuits hummed and throbbed and then Mary would let out a scream that would have woken the dead had there been any in their perfect world. Sometimes at breakfast one of the kids would say, "What was all that racket last night?" and another one would say, "That was Mom and Dad interfacing again," and there would be merry laughter all around the table.

They had three males and three females so the kids could have gone on interfacing among themselves but after a certain age it was considered desirable to couple outside the family circle and thereby expand the family network. The first to couple was Joanne. She brought Sid home just before the annual recitation of the history of the race. Sid also worked at the Information Center and was therefore thought of as a "good catch," belonging to their own class. John and Mary could see that Joanne was crazy about him because while they were eating she kept brushing against his chassis as though by accident.

"What division are you in?" John asked him.

"Commercial messages," Sid said.

"That must be exciting," Mary said.

"Sid designs the taste option ads," Joanne said.

"You sure convince me," Mary said. "I buy them all."

"It's what keeps the economy going," Sid said. "If there were no options we'd all be eating the same paste and there would be no growth and diversification."

"And fewer jobs at the Manufacturing Center," John added.

"Fewer jobs at the Information Center too," Sid said with a sly look.

"We'd have a recession," John said.

"Anyone care for some 'strawberry' jello?" Mary said.

After dinner they sat outside and John and Sid engaged in some more "shop talk" while Joanne looked at Sid adoringly and the other kids ran around in circles hitting a ball with a stick. The sky was clear and many stars were out as well as a full moon lit up by a distant sun that was said to be a star itself. Somewhere up there, everyone knew, there was a dead planet from which they themselves were said to have come, though there was some disagreement on the matter. Had they migrated from the dead planet, or was the dead planet in the red room as well? John certainly didn't know, though he knew almost everything else.

At the end of the evening Sid said, "I think I'll be floating along now," and Joanne accompanied him to the front gate, giving his cable an affectionate tug. When they were in bed, Mary said to John, "I hope it works out. He looks like a nice boy." John concurred.

After that they saw quite a lot of Sid, who'd come by nearly every evening to take Joanne out to a paste bar where young couples tried out a variety of stimulants and often came home with their memories gone. "Kids will be kids," Mary said. Fortunately it all worked out for the best. Sid and Joanne soon coupled and set up their own household. Needless to say, it wasn't long before the kids started to come. "A new generation," John sighed. They got the usual viruses and filled themselves with the cookies that Mary brought when she came over for a visit. One day Joanne said to Mary, "You know, Mom, the more we interface the more kids we get. There must be a connection."

"I don't think so," Mary said.

John didn't think so either. "The ideas kids get nowadays," he said.

"It was different when we were kids," Mary said.

"Remember the first time we interfaced?" John said.

Mary blushed. "How can I forget."

"I hardly knew what I was doing."

"You had the longest cable I had ever seen."

"It's a good thing your port was so big or I never would have gotten my plug in."

John was now a supervisor at the Information Center. It was rumored that he was in line to be moved to the center of the room to become a regulator and send out self-generated messages. That was as high as you could go in the system. All information was inside it. You worked with what you had, though there was a separate division for innovators who sometimes interfaced with external sources and forwarded astounding messages which John would have to sort and evaluate if he ever got his big promotion. Mary said she had a cousin in the higher echelons and it was well worth using her connections at this critical juncture in John's career to advance his interests but John said he preferred to have his case judged on its own merits and if worse came to worse he could transfer to the Service Center where there was always room at the top. "Anything but Manufacturing," Mary said. "You don't want to get stuck in straws."

In the end John got his promotion and was moved to the center of the room. It was a dream come true. He had achieved the highest position in the system. Everything came through him. He was at the heart of things. Mary threw a party. No one could refuse to come. She too was a force to be reckoned with now. She would no longer have to shop or clean the house or prepare her own pastes, and she could afford any straw that struck her fancy. These were going to be the best years of their lives lasting for a length of time that could not be measured. John sat in the center of the room and Mary threw more parties and was said to have the biggest collection of straws in the neighborhood. They also bought a flotation device so that they wouldn't have to exert themselves when they moved from place to place. Needless to say, they both put on a few extra pounds.

One by one the kids all coupled and moved away and suddenly they had the big house all to themselves again. In fact all the kids in the neighborhood had moved away by now so that the neighborhood looked more like a retirement village than anything else. They were all just starting to settle into middle age, which would last forever.

"I don't think I have the energy for another migration," Mary said.

"And all that packing," John said.

"What if we stayed behind."

"They'd have to deactivate us," John said, "and then we'd have to be upgraded when everyone got back."

"Why can't we just stay the way we are?"

"It doesn't work that way," John said. "You end up not being able to interface."

"But you and I could, if we stayed the same."

"What about the kids? It's more complicated than you think."

"But what happens if you don't deactivate?"

"There'd be no one here to service you. You'd end up on the scrap heap, like your old CPU."

"Sometimes I wonder if it's not for the best. After all, how long can you just go on?"

"Now now, Mary."

Clearly Mary was having another crisis so John took her to the Service Center again for a counseling session. The counselor asked her many intimate questions, like whether she was still secreting oil, and then gave her some powder to add to her paste. "This'll do the trick," the counselor said.

"What is it?" John said.

"Just a little pick-me-up."

Mary had wandered off again and John found her with her old CPU. "I wish you wouldn't," he said.

"I can't help it," Mary said.

"Let's go home."

"Give me another minute." When he was outside the storeroom he heard the familiar scream. He waited patiently and she came out looking somewhat sheepish.

John administered her powder faithfully but there was no improvement. Sometimes, when he got back from the Information Center, he found her sitting on the sofa just staring into space. Sometimes he heard her muttering to herself, "My old CPU, my old CPU, everything is there." This made no sense at all. What about all their years together? Did she want to just erase them?

"It's the menopause," a colleague said. "She'll get over it."

"But where do you go from there?" John said.

"Nowhere," his colleague said. "You just stay where you are."

"Forever?"

"Give or take a couple of years."

This was a big problem though the creatures of the red room did not like to admit it and were a little squeamish even about raising the subject. Occasionally someone pulled his own plug leaving notarized instructions not to be reactivated. They were generally consigned to the CPU storeroom in the Service Center with their moving parts going into the recycling bin. At the same time counselors devised all kinds of programs to keep the middle-aged occupied. Some played chess and some played checkers. Some interfaced promiscuously with thousands and thousands of partners, exposing the most intimate details of their lives and expressing opinions about every subject under the sun. This was considered even more debased than auto-degradation. Others watched TV from morning till night.

When it was time to retire John and Mary rented a smaller house and spent the mornings gardening, generally dozing off right after lunch. It wasn't much of a life and they were interfacing less and less now but somehow they got used to it and Mary had a facelift and general overhaul which picked up her spirits considerably. When it was finally time for the creatures of the red room to make their way back to their old nesting grounds, John and Mary were actually looking forward to opening the old house and getting back into harness. When they landed they saw that everything was just as they had left it and the lawn was still green. "Isn't this great," John said. In the evening they sat outside and had a drink. They were content. They had all of eternity to look forward to.

Fred Russell is the pen name of an American-born writer living in Israel. His novels *Rafi's World* (Fomite Press), dealing with Israel's emerging criminal class, and *The Links in the Chain* (CCLaP), a thriller set in New York against an Arab-Israel background, were both published in 2014. His stories and essays have appeared in *Third Coast, Polluto, Fiction on the Web, Wilderness House Literary Review, Ontologica, Unlikely Stories: Episode 4, The Satirist,* CounterPunch, *Gadfly, Cultural Weekly, Ragazine,* etc. Chapbook collections of his shorter opinion pieces called *Short Takes: American Notes* and *Short Takes II: Reviews and Opinions* appeared in 2015 and 2016.

Thank you to the Wapshott Press sponsors, supporters, and Friends of the Wapshott Press.

Muna Deriane
Ann Siemens
Suzanne Siegel
Debbie Jones
Steven Acker
Jennifer Bentson
Kathleen Bonagofsky
Carol Colin
Ted Waltz
Cynthia Henderson
Aubrey Hicks
Nancy Lilly
Jeff Morawetz
Patricia Nerad
Amanda Nerad
Elaine Padilla
Bradley Rader
Laurel Sutton
Deana Swart
Kathleen M. Warner

The Wapshott Press is a 501(c)(3) not-for-profit enterprise publishing work by emerging and established authors and artists. We publish books that should be published. We are very grateful to the people who believe in our plans and goals, as well as our hopes and dreams. Our new website is at www.WapshottPress.org